MY ADVENTURES

WITH

DISNEP

Princess Collection

This book was especially written for
Payson Noding
With love from
Dennis, Stephanie,
Mia, and Willow

D0096041

Believe in your dreams

Edited by Wendy Elks
ISBN 1 875676 19 8

MY ADVENTURES WITH CINDERELLA

Cinderella lived with her father, who loved her very much. He took her horseback riding and told her stories about castles and magic. One day he married again, but, not long afterwards, he died. Cinderella, left in the care of her Stepmother and two spoilt stepsisters, Drizella and Anastasia, was now a servant in her own home.

Payson Noding lived at 118 Elizabeth Avenue in Brick, New Jersey, not far from her friend Cinderella. One day, when she went to visit Cinderella, she found everyone in a state of great excitement.

'The King has invited all of the young women to a ball,' Cinderella told Payson. 'His son, the Prince, will be there. Drizella and Anastasia don't want me to go, but my Stepmother has said that I can if I finish all my chores.'

'How exciting!' said Payson. 'I'll help you!'

'Do you have a gown?' asked Payson. She knew that Cinderella's mean Stepmother rarely bought her any clothes.

'I have an old dress. With some fixing up, it will be fine,' said Cinderella.

The two friends worked very hard, cleaning and
helping the stepsisters to get ready. At last they
rushed to Cinderella's bedroom, high up in the
tower. There was hardly any time left to work on
Cinderella's old dress! To their surprise, dear Gus
and Jaq, and their friends the mice and birds, had
secretly turned it into a beautiful gown! Cinderella
slipped it on, and raced downstairs.

She looked so beautiful that her jealous
stepsisters tore the gown to shreds.

The wicked stepsisters and their mother left for the ball. Poor Cinderella ran out into the garden, and wept. Payson went with her, feeling very sad for her friend.

Suddenly a strange glow appeared in the garden. It was Cinderella's Fairy Godmother! Waving her magic wand, she turned a pumpkin into a magnificent coach and the mice into four beautiful horses!

Payson watched with disbelief as Cinderella's rags turned into a shimmering gown and on her feet appeared a pair of glass slippers that glittered like diamonds.

Cinderella and Payson climbed into the coach.

'There, off you go,' said the kindly Fairy Godmother. 'But beware you must return before the spell is broken, at the stroke of midnight.'

When they arrived at the palace, Cinderella ran up the stairs and was swept into a dream world.

Everyone stared at the beautiful girl but not even her family knew who she was. The Prince couldn't take his eyes off Cinderella. They danced together all evening, falling deeply in love.

Payson watched from the balcony and she wished that her friends, Mia, Georgia and Willow could also be there to enjoy the magical evening.

Later on, the Prince and Cinderella walked in the Palace gardens and found Payson. Cinderella wanted her friend to meet the Prince. Payson was so shy she could barely speak! But he was very kind. The Prince asked her when her birthday was. She told him it was on November 18th. 'Did you know that your birthstone is a topaz?' he asked as he took a beautiful jewel out of his pocket and gave it to Payson.

The Prince and Cinderella went inside and danced again. Suddenly, it was close to midnight and Cinderella raced down the grand staircase. In her haste she lost one of her glass slippers.

On the way home, the magic wore off and the coach turned back into a pumpkin, and the horses became mice again.

'Oh, Payson, what a wonderful night!' sighed Cinderella.

'You looked so beautiful, Cinderella,' said Payson. 'And you still have your glass slipper to remember it by!'

'Yes, and you still have your beautiful topaz!' said Cinderella. 'Now we both have mementos of an enchanted evening.'

The next day the Prince sent the Grand Duke in search of the mysterious young woman who'd danced with the Prince. When he called at their house with the glass slipper, Cinderella's Stepmother locked her in her room! Drizella and Anastasia tried to force their feet into the slipper but it didn't fit.

Somehow Cinderella's friends Gus and Jaq were able to free her and she ran downstairs. Suddenly, she heard a crash and saw that the slipper brought by the Grand Duke was broken! Pulling the other slipper from her pocket, she slipped it onto her foot. It proved she was the one they were looking for.

Soon it was announced that Cinderella and the Prince were getting married. There was a beautiful wedding at the Palace. Payson was there too, as a flowergirl. Cinderella wanted her friend, who had helped her so much, to be part of her special day.

Cinderella was now a Princess, and sometimes Payson went to the Palace to visit and occasionally, Mia, Georgia and Willow went too!

MY ADVENTURES WITH SLEEPING BEAUTY

Once upon a time, a baby girl was born to a King and Queen. They called her Aurora. Everyone loved her, except for the wicked fairy, Maleficent, who cast a spell on her. Before the sun sets on her sixteenth birthday, Aurora would prick her finger on the spindle of a spinning wheel, and die. The good fairy, Merryweather, managed to change the spell so that Aurora would fall asleep rather than die. She could be awakened by a kiss of love.

To protect Aurora from Maleficent, the King and Queen sent her into hiding with the three good fairies, Flora, Fauna and Merryweather. Nobody would expect the fairies to live in the forest and raise the child themselves.

Payson and her friends, Mia, Georgia and Willow were playing deep in the forest with Briar Rose and her many animal and bird friends. Briar Rose was always happy, and dreaming of the day when she would meet a handsome prince, and fall in love.

Today was a special day. It was November 18th, Briar Rose's 16th birthday *and* Payson's birthday. They were all having such fun. The animals had dressed up, and were pretending to be the handsome stranger in Briar Rose's dreams. Suddenly, a handsome stranger *did* come along and he joined Briar Rose in a beautiful song. It seemed to Payson that they were falling in love as they danced and sang!

Briar Rose invited the young man to the cottage for dinner that evening. Soon, it was time to go and she and her friends went back to the cottage to tell the fairies. They had always warned her not to talk to strangers, but this man wasn't a stranger - he was the man of her dreams!

Flora, Fauna and Merryweather were very upset. The time had come to tell her the truth. They told Briar Rose that her real name was Aurora, and that she was a princess!

They also told her that she was to return to the castle and marry the son of King Hubert. This would unite their kingdoms.

'But I don't want to marry someone I've never met before, even if he is a prince!' cried Aurora. 'I love the man I met in the forest!'

'You can never see him again,' said Fauna sadly. 'Tonight, we must return to the castle to meet your father, King Stefan.'

Mia, Georgia and Willow had to go home, but Payson was allowed to go with Aurora and the fairies.

'I'm so glad you're with me, Payson,' Aurora said, as they walked through the forest. 'It's exciting being a princess. But I don't want to marry King Hubert's son - I've never even met him!'

'Perhaps he's very nice,' said Payson. 'And it will be fun, living in a castle.'

Afraid of being discovered by Maleficent before sundown, the fairies smuggled Aurora into the castle. She sat in her new bedroom, thinking about the handsome stranger she'd met in the forest. He would go to the cottage, and find no one there.

Then she thought about how wonderful it was
to have a mother and father. They had lived
without her for all these years, so that she would
be safe from Maleficent.

A strange green light appeared in her room.
Aurora fell under its spell. She followed the light
up a staircase and into a dark room, where there
was a magic spinning wheel. Aurora touched the
spindle, and instantly fell asleep. Maleficent was
triumphant - her spell had worked!

Payson was tired after the long walk, and had fallen asleep on Aurora's bed. When she woke up and found Aurora gone, she felt scared.

Suddenly Merryweather flew into the room. 'Aurora has pricked her finger and fallen asleep!' she cried. 'Everyone else in the land will go to sleep too, until Aurora is awakened!'

'How can she wake up?' wondered Payson.

'Only true love's kiss can do it,' said Merryweather.

'Then we should find the man in the forest,' said Payson. 'I'm sure he loves Aurora.'

Just then, Flora came in. 'I overheard King Stefan saying that Prince Phillip is insisting on marrying a peasant girl. Could it be that he is the young man from the forest?'

'Quick we must go back to the cottage to find him,' cried Flora.

When they arrived, they discovered that he wasn't there. Maleficent had captured him and taunted him with the news that only he could awaken Aurora with a kiss.

They raced to the Forbidden Mountains where Maleficent lived. They crept down to the dungeon, and Flora, Fauna and Merryweather freed Phillip.

'I must go and save her!' he cried.

Flora conjured up the Sword of Truth and the Shield of Virtue, so that Phillip could fight Maleficent and her powers of evil.

Phillip mounted his horse and headed for the castle where his beautiful Aurora lay sleeping. The good fairies flew after him. Flora and Fauna held Payson's hands, and she flew, too! High over the forest they went. It was the most exciting thing she had ever done!

Bravely, Phillip fought Maleficent. She turned herself into a dragon and blasted him with red-hot flames. With the help of the fairies' magic, he hurled the Sword of Truth at the dragon and cut her down.

Phillip ran through the gates of the castle and entered the chamber where Aurora lay sleeping. He bent to kiss her, and watched her open her eyes.

The whole Kingdom woke up. Prince Phillip and Aurora came down the stairs, and Aurora ran into the arms of her parents, reunited at last.

The celebrations began. Hundreds of guests from all over the kingdom arrived to see the happy couple marry. King Stefan and King Hubert toasted the royal couple who had met once upon a dream.

MY ADVENTURES WITH THE LITTLE MERMAID

Payson Noding's birthday is November 18th. To celebrate, Payson's family and friends, Mia, Georgia and Willow went to a magical beach where it was always sunny and the water was warm and sparkling.

While she was swimming, Payson met Ariel, a mermaid who lived in Atlantica. Payson thought that Ariel was special because she could swim so fast, and had a beautiful singing voice. Ariel thought that Payson was special, because she was human, and could run and dance.

'I've always wanted to be human,' Ariel said. 'When I was a girl I used to collect things made by humans. I would watch ships pass by and spy on humans on the beach so that I could learn about these two-legged creatures. My father, King Triton, told me that humans were cruel and that I should stay away from them.'

'Not long ago, I saved a man from a shipwreck. His name is Prince Eric. I fell in love with him, and now I want to be human more than ever.'

Suddenly, Ariel started to cry.

'What's wrong?' asked Payson, who hated to see her new friend upset. 'Maybe I can help you.'

'Father heard that I had rescued Prince Eric and got very angry. He destroyed all the human treasures I'd collected! I was so upset I made a deal with Ursula, the Sea Witch, and it has all gone wrong,' sobbed Ariel.

Payson put her arm around Ariel. 'What happened?' she asked kindly.

'Ursula said that if I gave her my voice, she would make me human for three days,' Ariel explained. 'If Prince Eric kissed me by sunset on the third day, I would stay human. If not, I would belong to the Sea Witch. I agreed, and suddenly I was on a beach, and I had legs! Prince Eric found me and took me back to his palace. We had two wonderful days together. Then, on the third day, I learned that Eric had fallen in love with someone else and they were to marry on Eric's ship! My friend, Scuttle, the seagull, discovered that it was Ursula, disguised as a girl with a beautiful voice - my voice!'

'Scuttle and his friends burst in on the wedding ceremony. In the chaos, Ursula's necklace that held my voice fell to the ground and broke, and my voice flowed back to me. But it was too late. The sun had set and I changed back into a mermaid. I belonged to Ursula. She took me back to my father who insisted that she take him, instead of me. Now, Ursula is Ruler of the Sea, and my father, her slave.'

'Payson, will you help me free my father, and get our kingdom back?' asked Ariel.

Payson was happy to help her friend. She waved to Mia, Georgia and Willow. Payson and Ariel swam out to sea to find Ursula.

When they found Ursula, they discovered that,
with the magic of King Triton's trident, she had
made herself enormous and she towered over
Eric's ship. She was angry and jealous of the
love Ariel and Eric had for each other.

With her huge tentacles, she created a giant
whirlpool that made the seas ferocious.
A gigantic wave washed Eric from the deck of his
ship and threw him on to a shipwreck that had
floated to the surface in the swirling sea. Ariel
watched horrified, as Eric tried to make his way
to the wheel of the old wreck.

Payson and Ariel shouted at Ursula and tried desperately to hold her attention. Eric grabbed hold of the wheel of the ship and steered the bow right into Ursula's black heart.

Together, Payson, Ariel and Eric defeated the Sea Witch!

Payson and Ariel swam down to Ursula's cave where they found King Triton. They returned his trident to him and his power was restored!

King Triton forgave Ariel for causing so much trouble. Realizing that she really did love Eric, he granted his daughter her greatest wish and transformed her tail into legs again! Now Ariel could marry her prince!

'You're my first human friend, Payson - apart from Eric, of course,' said Ariel. 'And you must come back for our wedding which, in your honor, will be held on November 18th.'

Payson was so happy that she had been able to help her friend and promised that she would return for the wedding.

   With King Triton's blessing, Ariel and Eric were
married and what had once been two worlds
became one kingdom.

   Ariel, who was once a little mermaid, became a
princess of both land and sea.

This personalized Disney Princess book was specially created for Payson Noding of 118 Elizabeth Avenue, Brick, New Jersey with love from Dennis, Stephanie, Mia, and Willow.

Additional books ordered may be mailed separately - please allow a few days for differences in delivery times.

If you would like to receive additional My Adventure Book order forms, please contact:

My Adventure Books
Email: inquiry@identitydirect.com
www.identitydirect.com

0864 002806 000201 DM 191